Hello, Family Members,

Learning to read is one of the most important accomplishments of early childhood. **Hello Reader!** books are designed to help children become skilled readers who like to read. Beginning readers learn to read by remembering frequently used words like "the," "is," and "and"; by using phonics skills to decode new words; and by interpreting picture and text clues. These books provide both the stories children enjoy and the structure they need to read fluently and independently. Here are suggestions for helping your child *before*, *during*, and *after* reading:

Before

- Look at the cover and pictures and have your child predict what the story is about.
- Read the story to your child.
- Encourage your child to chime in with familiar words and phrases.
- Echo read with your child by reading a line first and having your child read it after you do.

During

- Have your child think about a word he or she does not recognize right away. Provide hints such as "Let's see if we know the sounds" and "Have we read other words like this one?"
- Encourage your child to use phonics skills to sound out new words.
- Provide the word for your child when more assistance is needed so that he or she does not struggle and the experience of reading with you is a positive one.
- Encourage your child to have fun by reading with a lot of expression...like an actor!

After

- Have your child keep lists of interesting and favorite words.
- Encourage your child to read the books over and over again. Have him or her read to brothers, sisters, grandparents, and even teddy bears. Repeated readings develop confidence in young readers.
- Talk about the stories. Ask and answer questions. Share ideas about the funniest and most interesting characters and events in the stories.

I do hope that you and your child enjoy this book.

— Francie Alexander
  Chief Education Officer,
  Scholastic's Learning Ventures

D1611417

For Nicole Kelly, better late than never!
— K.M.

To my sister, Karen.
— M.S.

ISBN 0-439-31942-0

Text copyright © 2001 by Kate McMullan.
Illustrations copyright © 2001 by Mavis Smith.
All rights reserved. Published by Scholastic Inc.
SCHOLASTIC, HELLO READER, CARTWHEEL BOOKS,
and associated logos are trademarks and/or
registered trademarks of Scholastic Inc.

Library of Congress Cataloging-in-Publication Data

McMullan, Kate.
    Fluffy, the secret Santa / by Kate McMullan ; illustrated by Mavis Smith.
        p. cm. — (Hello reader! Level 3)
    "Cartwheel books."
    Summary: At Christmastime Fluffy the class guinea pig discovers that he likes both getting presents and giving them.
        ISBN: 0-439-31942-0 (pbk.)
        [1. Guinea pigs—Fiction. 2. Christmas—Fiction. 3. Schools—Fiction.]
I. Smith, Mavis, ill. II. Title. III. Series.

PZ7.M2295 Ffe 2001
[E]—dc21   2001032254

10 9 8 7 6 5 4 3 2 1   01 02 03 04 05

Printed in the U.S.A.   24
First printing, November 2001

FLUFFY
THE SECRET SANTA

by Kate McMullan
Illustrated by Mavis Smith

Hello Reader! — Level 3

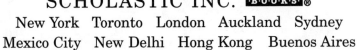

SCHOLASTIC INC.

Cartwheel
·B·O·O·K·S·®

New York   Toronto   London   Auckland   Sydney
Mexico City   New Delhi   Hong Kong   Buenos Aires

Secret Santa Fluffy

The week before winter break,
Ms. Day put on a Santa hat.
"Guess what, class?" she said.
"You get to be Secret Santas
for the kindergarten kids this year!"
Secret what? thought Fluffy.

"We had Secret Santas
when we were in kindergarten,"
said Wade. "Our Secret Santas
left us little presents every day
for a week."
Presents? thought Fluffy.
Count me in!

Ms. Day put the names of the kindergarten kids into her Santa hat. Everyone picked a name.

Pass the hat to me! thought Fluffy.
I want to be a Secret Santa, too.
"Did everyone pick a name?"
asked Ms. Day.
Not this pig, thought Fluffy.

"Ms. Day?" said Jasmine.
"Can Fluffy be a Secret Santa
for Lucky Sue, the kindergarten
guinea pig?"
Ms. Day smiled. "Why not?" she said.
All right! thought Fluffy.
Bring on the presents!

"Fluffy can give Lucky Sue
lots of presents," said Wade.
GIVE? thought Fluffy.
Hold it right there.

Wade and Jasmine went over
to Fluffy's cage.
"What should Lucky Sue's first
present be?" said Jasmine.
"Fluffy could give her this
coconut shell," said Wade.
Give away my coconut shell?
thought Fluffy. **Not a chance!**

"How about his chew stick?"
said Jasmine.
Nobody touches my chew stick!
thought Fluffy.
"It's too icky," said Wade.
It is? thought Fluffy.

"Let's have Fluffy give
Lucky Sue his rock," said Wade.
No! thought Fluffy. **Not my rock!**
But Wade took Fluffy's rock
and wrapped it up.

Later, Ms. Day's class
handed out gifts
to the kindergarten kids.
The kids got picture frames
the class had made for them.
Lucky Sue got Fluffy's rock.

Wade and Jasmine came back
to Fluffy's cage the next day.
"What can Secret Santa Fluffy
give Lucky Sue today?" asked Wade.
What!? thought Fluffy.
She needs *another* present?
"How about his treats?" said Wade.
You must be joking! thought Fluffy.
But Jasmine and Wade wrapped up the
treat box. They took it to Lucky Sue.

The next morning, Jasmine and
Wade came to Fluffy's cage again.
But Fluffy was ready for them.
He had hidden his toys
under his cardboard fort.
Heh-heh, thought Fluffy.

"Do you think Lucky Sue would like to have Fort Fluffy?" said Jasmine.
She wouldn't! thought Fluffy.
But Wade picked up Fort Fluffy.

He and Jasmine wrapped it up
to give to Lucky Sue.
"Fluffy," said Jasmine,
"you're a good Secret Santa."
Where will it all end?
thought Fluffy.

Thank You, Fluffy!

On Friday, the kindergarten class
gave a party.
They asked their Secret Santas
to come for juice and cookies.
"Secret Santa Fluffy," said Wade,
"you can come, too."
Do I have to? said Fluffy.

Wade carried Fluffy to the
kindergarten room.
He put him in Lucky Sue's cage.
Lucky Sue was napping.
Fluffy looked around.
He could not believe what he saw!

His rock was in Lucky Sue's
food bowl. Bits of food were
stuck all over it.
Yuck! thought Fluffy.

Fluffy saw his treat box.
He ran over to it and
looked inside. It was empty.
She ate them ALL! thought Fluffy.

Fluffy saw his fort. At least
he thought it was his fort.
But it was hard to tell.
Lucky Sue had chewed it to bits.
Fort Fluffy! thought Fluffy. **Gone!**
How I used to like curling up
inside it with my chew stick.

"Wake up, Lucky Sue," said Wade.

"Here is your Secret Santa!"

Lucky Sue's eyes popped open.

She looked at Fluffy.

YOU were my Secret Santa?

said Lucky Sue.

The one and only, said Fluffy.

Lucky Sue jumped up.

She ran to Fluffy.

She threw her arms around him.

Oh! I love my presents! she said.

You do? said Fluffy.

Oh, yes! said Lucky Sue. **I do!**

I am a lucky Lucky Sue!

Lucky Sue ran over to the rock.
**See how pretty the rock
looks in my food bowl?** she asked.
Fluffy nodded. **I guess,** he said.

And those treats! said Lucky Sue.

Fluffy sighed. **Yeah,** he said.

I liked them myself.

Lucky Sue twirled with joy.

**Oh! I have never eaten such
yummy treats!** she said.

Thank you, Secret Santa Fluffy!

Fluffy shrugged.

I knew you'd like those treats,
he said.

Lucky Sue ran over to
what was left of Fort Fluffy.
She picked up a piece of it.
And this! she said. **I have never**
chewed such crunchy cardboard!
She took a bite. *CRUNCH!*

Fluffy picked up a piece
of the fort. He bit into it.
Lucky Sue was right.
It was fine, crunchy cardboard.
I'm glad I gave this to a pig
who likes a good crunch,
said Fluffy.

Lucky Sue twirled some more.

Oh, Fluffy! she said.

You gave me such beautiful presents!

Fluffy smiled.

I was glad to do it, he said.

You are the world's BEST Secret Santa! said Lucky Sue.

The best? said Fluffy.

Do you really think so?

Secret Presents

When the party was over,
Wade and Jasmine came over
to Lucky Sue's cage.
"Secret Santa has to go home,
Lucky Sue," Wade said.
Good-bye! Good-bye! said Lucky Sue.

Jasmine carried Fluffy back to
the classroom. When the kids
walked into the room, they saw
a little present on every desk.
"Wow!" said Wade.
"Secret Santa has been here!"

The kids opened their presents.
Secret Santa gave them each
a little wind-up monster.
"Cool!" said Maxwell.

"Look," said Jasmine. "Secret Santa
brought Fluffy a present, too."
He did? thought Fluffy.
Then he saw a box in his cage.
It was wrapped in brown paper.
It had a big straw bow.
He did! thought Fluffy.

Jasmine put Fluffy into his cage.

He started chewing the brown paper.

He chewed the straw ribbon.

And the bow. He chewed and chewed.

At last the paper fell away.

And Fluffy saw his present.

It was a cardboard castle!
"I guess that makes you
a king, Fluffy," said Wade.
You may bow, thought King Fluffy.

Fluffy ran into his castle.

There was a branch inside.

He sank his teeth into it.

He pulled it out through the door.

"You have a new chew stick, Fluffy,"
said Jasmine.

Oh, yum! thought Fluffy.

He could hardly wait
to give it a good chew.

"Secret Santa left this
for you, too," said Ms. Day.
She put half a red pepper filled with
green peas into his food bowl.
Oh, boy! Oh, boy! thought Fluffy.
He felt as lucky as Lucky Sue.

Fluffy ate a few peas.

He nibbled his red pepper.

He chewed on his new chew stick.

He ran in and out of Castle Fluffy
again and again.

I am a pig who likes presents,
thought Fluffy. **I like getting them.**
But giving them is fun, too.
He wasn't sure which he liked best.

"Ms. Day?" said Wade.
"Who was our Secret Santa?"
"It's a secret," said Ms. Day.
"Maybe it was Secret Santa Fluffy,"
said Jasmine.

You never know, thought Fluffy.
**After all, I have been called
the world's BEST Secret Santa.**